W9-BIT-751

MBJ

The Swollen Fox

Why should you share with others?

www.av2books.com

ANIMATED STORYTIME
AV²
BY WEIGL™
ADDED VALUE • AUDIO VISUAL
POP CORN
ADMIT ONE

Go to **www.av2books.com**, and enter this book's unique code.

BOOK CODE

B815105

AV² by Weigl brings you media enhanced books that support active learning.

Published by AV² by Weigl
350 5th Avenue, 59th Floor New York, NY 10118
Websites: www.av2books.com   www.weigl.com

Library of Congress Cataloging-in-Publication Data

The swollen fox / Aesop.
     pages cm. -- (Storytime)
  Summary: "In The Swollen Fox, Aesop and his troupe teach their audience the value of sharing. They learn that it is important to take only what you need"-- Provided by publisher.
  ISBN 978-1-4896-2443-7 (hardcover : alk. paper) -- ISBN 978-1-4896-2444-4 (single user ebook) -- ISBN 978-1-4896-2445-1 (multi user ebook)
 [1. Fables. 2. Folklore.] I. Aesop.
 PZ8.2.S98 2014
 398.2--dc23
 [E]
                                              2014009680

Printed in the United States in North Mankato, Minnesota
1 2 3 4 5 6 7 8 9 0 18 17 16 15 14

052014
WEP090514

2

FABLE SYNOPSIS

J398.
2
SWO
C.1

For thousands of years, parents and teachers have used memorable stories called fables to teach simple moral lessons to children.

In the Aesop's Fables by AV² series, classic fables are given a lighthearted twist. These familiar tales are performed by a troupe of animal players whose endearing personalities bring the stories to life.

In *The Swollen Fox*, Aesop and his troupe teach their audience the value of sharing. They learn that it is important to take only what you need.

This AV² media enhanced book comes alive with...

Animated Video
Watch a custom animated movie.

Try This!
Complete activities and hands-on experiments.

Key Words
Study vocabulary, and complete a matching word activity.

Quiz
Test your knowledge.

The Swollen FOX

Why should you share with others?

AV² Storytime Navigation

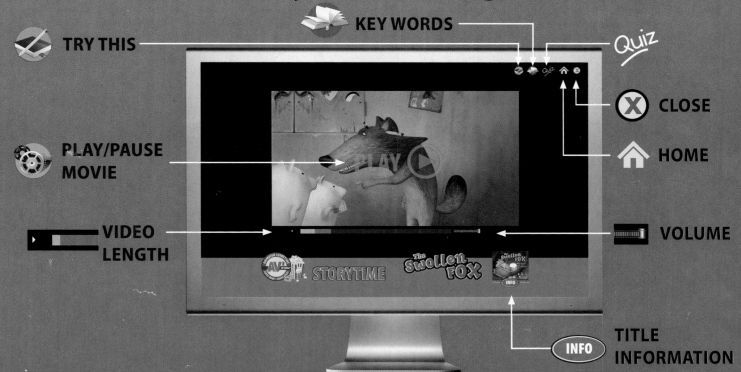

TRY THIS

KEY WORDS

Quiz

CLOSE

PLAY/PAUSE MOVIE

HOME

VIDEO LENGTH

VOLUME

INFO · **TITLE INFORMATION**

3

The Players

Aesop
I am the leader of Aesop's Theater, a screenwriter, and an actor.
I can be hot-tempered, but I am also soft and warm-hearted.

Libbit
I am an actor and a prop man.
I think I should have been a lion, but I was born a rabbit.

Presy
I am the manager of Aesop's Theater.
I am also the narrator of the plays.

4

The Story

The Shorties were very excited.

They had found a candy jar in Aesop's office.

They were trying to reach the jar, but it was too high.

The Shorties came up with a plan.

Bogart and Elvis piled books onto a chair.

Then, they lay down on top of the books.

Goddard climbed to the top and reached up high!

He could almost reach the jar.

9

Goddard stretched out for the jar.

He was able to pull the jar to the edge of the shelf.

Suddenly, the jar slipped from his hand and dropped.

Luckily, Libbit caught the jar.

He took out a candy and ate it.

The Shorties rushed towards Libbit.

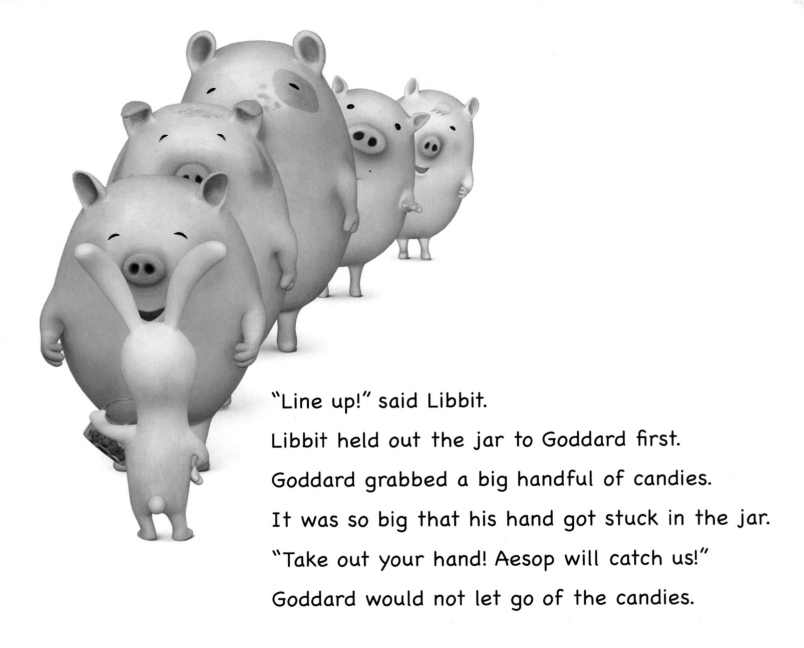

"Line up!" said Libbit.

Libbit held out the jar to Goddard first.

Goddard grabbed a big handful of candies.

It was so big that his hand got stuck in the jar.

"Take out your hand! Aesop will catch us!"

Goddard would not let go of the candies.

Just then, Aesop opened the door.

"Why is your hand in the candy jar?" asked Aesop.

Goddard looked guilty.

He held out his hand for Aesop to see.

Aesop laughed. "Silly Goddard! Your hand is stuck because you are too greedy!"

15

"If you let go of the candies,

you'll be able to pull your hand out!" said Aesop.

Still, Goddard would not let go of the candies.

"Don't be greedy, Goddard!" said Libbit. "We want candy, too!"

Presy had a wonderful idea.

"Goddard, if you give up the candies, I will tell you a story."

Goddard took his time thinking about the offer.

Finally, he decided to let go of the candies.

"This story is called *The Swollen Fox*," said Presy.

One day, a hungry fox was looking for food.

"I'm so hungry that I can't walk any farther."

Then, the fox smelled something yummy.

He found a farmer's meal in a tree hole.

The fox slipped into the hole and started eating.

21

The fox tried to leave after finishing his meal.

Sadly, the fox was now too big to get out of the hole.

"Oh no! What if the farmer finds me!" said the fox.

A second fox was passing by and saw the first fox.

The first fox explained what had happened.

"Don't worry," said the second fox. "You are big now.

When you shrink again, you will get out easily."

Luckily, the farmer did not come.

The fox was able to leave the hole late that night.

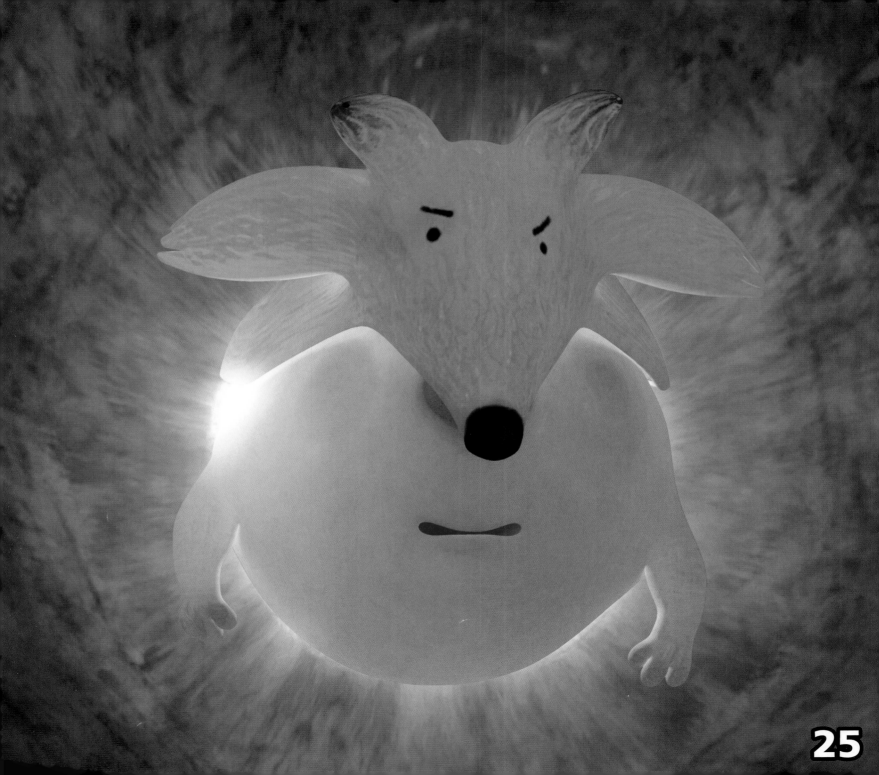

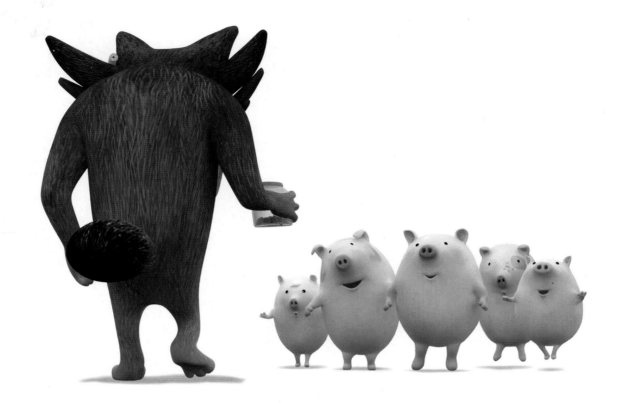

Aesop gathered the Shorties.

"You can each take one candy from the jar."

Goddard put his hand into the jar.

He took out only one candy.

"Good job, Goddard! You learned your lesson," said Aesop.

It is always best to share. If you take more
than you need, you may find yourself in trouble.

What is a Story?

Players

Who is the story about? The characters, or players, are the people, animals, or objects that perform the story. Characters have personality traits that contribute to the story. Readers understand how a character fits into the story by what the character says and does, what others say about the character, and how others treat the character.

Setting

Where and when do the events take place? The setting of a story helps readers visualize where and when the story is taking place. These details help to suggest the mood or atmosphere of the story. A setting is usually presented briefly, but it explains whether the story is taking place in the past, present, or future and in a large or small area.

Plot

What happens in the story? The plot is a story's plan of action. Most plots follow a pattern. They begin with an introduction and progress to the rising action of events. The events lead to a climax, which is the most exciting moment in the story. The resolution is the falling action of events. This section ties up loose ends so that readers are not left with unanswered questions. The story ends with a conclusion that brings the events to a close.

Point of View

Who is telling the story? The story is normally told from the point of view of the narrator, or storyteller. The narrator can be a main character or a less important character in the story. He or she can also be someone who is not in the story but is observing the action. This observer may be impartial or someone who knows the thoughts and feelings of the characters. A story can also be told from different points of view.

Dialogue

What type of conversation occurs in the story? Conversation, or dialogue, helps to show what is happening. It also gives information about the characters. The reader can discover what kinds of people they are by the words they say and how they say them. Writers use dialogue to make stories more interesting. In dialogue, writers imitate the way real people speak, so it is written differently than the rest of the story.

Theme

What is the story's underlying meaning? The theme of a story is the topic, idea, or position that the story presents. It is often a general statement about life. Sometimes, the theme is stated clearly. Other times, it is suggested through hints.

The Swollen Fox Quiz

1 What was on the shelf?

2 What did the Shorties use to reach the candy jar?

3 Who caught the candy jar after it fell?

4 What did the fox find in a tree?

5 Why could the fox not get out of the hole?

6 How many candies did Aesop offer the Shorties?

Key Words

Research has shown that as much as 65 percent of all written material published in English is made up of 300 words. These 300 words cannot be taught using pictures or learned by sounding them out. They must be recognized by sight. This book contains 116 common sight words to help young readers improve their reading fluency and comprehension. This book also teaches young readers several important content words, such as proper nouns. These words are paired with pictures to aid in learning and improve understanding.

Page	Sight Words First Appearance
4	a, also, am, an, and, be, been, but, can, have, I, of, plays, should, the, think, was
5	always, animals, at, do, food, from, get, good, if, like, never, other, them, to, very, want, with
6	found, had, high, in, it, they, too, were
9	almost, came, could, down, on, then, up
11	for, hand, he, his, out, took
12	big, first, go, got, let, line, not, said, so, take, that, us, will, would, your
15	are, asked, because, is, just, see, why, you
16	don't, still, we
19	about, give, idea, story, tell, this, time
20	any, day, into, one, something, started
23	after, leave, me, no, now, what
24	again, by, come, did, night, saw, second, when
26	each, find, may, more, need, only, put, than

Page	Content Words First Appearance
4	actor, leader, lion, manager, narrator, prop man, rabbit, screenwriter, theater
5	dance, music, pig
6	candy jar, jar
9	books, chair
11	candy, shelf
15	door
19	fox
20	farmer's meal, tree hole
23	farmer, meal

Check out av2books.com for your animated storytime media enhanced book!

1 Go to av2books.com

2 Enter book code B 8 1 5 1 0 5

3 Fuel your imagination online!

www.av2books.com

AV² Storytime Navigation

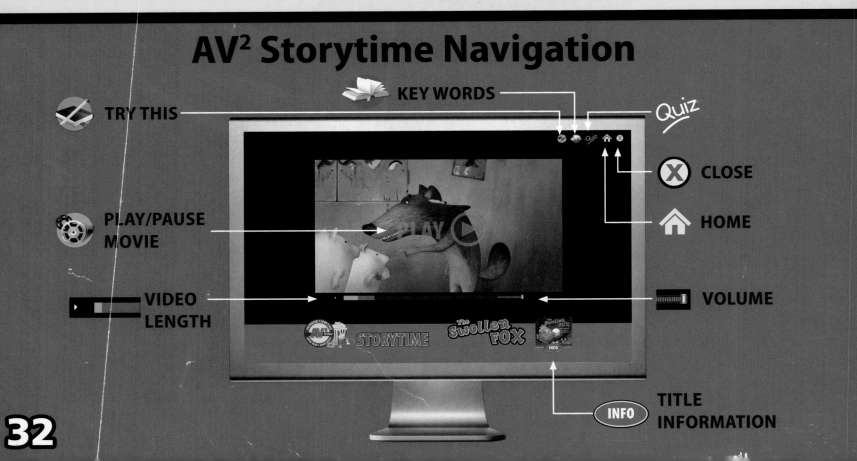

KEY WORDS

Quiz

TRY THIS

X CLOSE

PLAY/PAUSE MOVIE

HOME

VIDEO LENGTH

VOLUME

INFO TITLE INFORMATION